The Story of 1000 ANTS & The Sleepy GENERAL

Goal Standard
PUBLISHING

A Sleep Meditation Tale for
Restless Children & Exhausted Parents

By: Edward deGuia

_____

This book belongs to:

The Story of 1000 ANTS & The Sleepy GENERAL

Goal Standard
PUBLISHING

The Story of 1000 Ants & The Sleepy General, 2568 Seven Kings Road, Virginia Beach, VA 23456.

Recommended for children aged 2 years and over. Conforms to safety requirements of CPSIA and ASTM

Library of Congress Control No. 2020950234

Library of Congress Cataloguing in Publication Data

Names: DeGuia, Edward, 1975 - author.

Title: The story of 1000 ants & the sleepy general : a sleep meditation tale for restless children & exhausted parents / by: Edward deGuia.

Description: Virginia Beach, VA : Goal Standard Publishing, [2020] | A QR code inside of the book, when accessed, leads to 2 hours of sleep meditation music online. | Audience: K-1, ages 2-6. | Summary: Is your little one having trouble falling asleep at bedtime? With the use of this book, you will encourage your child to have a more meaningful sleep. "The Story of 1000 Ants and The Sleepy General" explores mindfulness with your child to help manage stress, emotions while navigating personal challenges. This fun-loving story follows a sleepy General as he commands his troops to complete the mission of retrieving a cake from the picnic table in the park. This story is sure to entertain your child and slow them to a comfort that will allow your baby to rest comfortably throughout the night. The General includes two free hours of sleep meditation music that may be played while reading the story or not. The included bonus music is sure to lull your baby to sleep. --Publisher.

Identifiers: ISBN: 978-1-953941-00-8 (hardcover) | 978-1-953941-01-5 (paperback) | 978-1-953941-02-2 (ebook) | LCCN: 2020950234

Subjects: LCSH: Bedtime--Juvenile fiction. | Sleep--Juvenile fiction. | Ants--Juvenile fiction. | Generals--Juvenile fiction. | Mindfulness (Psychology)--Juvenile fiction. | Stress management for children--Juvenile fiction. | CYAC: Bedtime--Fiction. | Sleep--Fiction. | Ants--Fiction | Stress management--Fiction.

Classification: LCC: PZ7.1.D449 S76 2020 | DDC: [E]--dc23

MADE IN USA

To my wife Lani and our amazing children Jaelyn, Rena, Apollo, Demaris, and Amado

Thank you for your love and support for my pursuits through the years. It wasn't always easy, but it was always done with love and the family in mind.

SCAN ME

← Free Music Download

HOW TO USE

Before beginning the story...

☆ **Develop a routine that lasts 30 minutes or less, not including bath time which should take place within 1 hour of bedtime.** Some routine tasks will include brushing teeth, putting on PJs, eating a light snack and reading this story with your child tucked into bed.

☆ **Ensure the room temperature is cool but not cold, quiet and free of distracting electronic devices.**

☆ **Scan the QR Code on the left side to que the sleepy meditation music once you and your child are ready to read.** Once your child is sound asleep you may allow the music to continue or turn off.

GENERAL
ANT ARMY

THIS BOOK

NOTE: This story is designed to never end.

Essentially, the counting portion of the story will repeat itself several times until your child is asleep (Much like counting sheep present day).

With each time you are prompted to restart; begin reading more slowly, take deeper breaths between the numbers and yawn even more.

Always count in a slow monotone voice.

ENJOY!

The queen ant saw the chocolate cake from afar. It had fresh cherries spread all over.

The queen decided to organize the ants to get some cake.

So the tired general followed orders

and returned to the troops exhausted from his time with the queen.

He was so sleepy.

The ants were eager to help and wanted to get the cake.

Breathing slowly; the general's voice begins to gradually fade as he continued the count.

The general was getting tired as he counted.

He was getting tired and decided to rest.

He stopped for a moment and thought about his mission.

When he returned to count the ants, he forgot where he stopped.

So the General, took a moment, yawned, and took a deep breath.

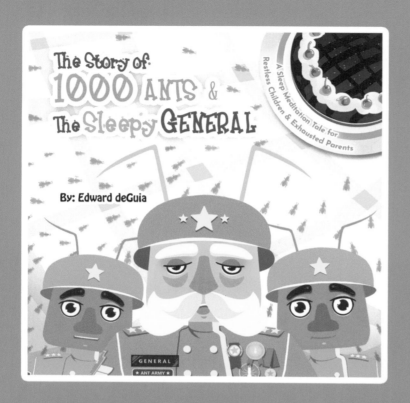

🌐 thestoryof1000ants.com

✉️ ed.deguia.books@gmail.com

f The Story of 1000 Ants

ABOUT THE AUTHOR

Edward N. deGuia, M.B.A., BSN, RN

Edward is an enthusiastic leader that values communication in organizational development and personal development. Starting his career as a pediatric nurse while serving in the U.S. Navy, Edward has valued communicating with people at the right station in their lives. His background in nursing and consulting have provided him numerous opportunities to engage and communicate with fellow staff, leadership, and clients.

Health and wellbeing are very important. Mindfulness and wellness need an approach that is communicated at the proper level. With constant activity in their lives, children must learn the proper mindset to begin to rest. Edward has told the story of 1,000 ants to his children countless times to ease their mind to a resting state. **Utilizing techniques often found in meditation, Edward brings this book in hopes to help your child rest the mind to find better sleep.**

Goal Standard

PUBLISHING

A Division of BJ Hernandez Books

Have a book idea?

Contact us at:

🌐 goalstandardpublishing.com

✉ info@goalstandardpublishing.com

CPSIA information can be obtained
at www.ICGtesting.com
Printed in the USA
LVHW071557070121
675999LV00010B/241